Welcome to ALADDIN QUIX!

If you are looking for fast, fun-to-read stories with colorful characters, lots of kid-friendly humor, easy-to-follow action, entertaining story lines, and lively illustrations, then **ALADDIN QUIX** is for you!

But wait, there's more!

If you're also looking for stories with tables of contents; word lists; about-the-book questions; 64, 80, or 96 pages; short chapters; short paragraphs; and large fonts, then **ALADDIN QUIX** is *definitely* for you!

ALADDIN QUIX: The next step between ready to reads and longer, more challenging chapter books, for readers five to eight years old.

Stars of the Show

The Adventures of ALLIE and AMY

Stars of the Show

By Stephanie Calmenson and Joanna Cole
Illustrated by James Burks

ALADDIN QUIX

New York London Toronto Sydney New Delhi

ALADDIN QUIX
Simon & Schuster Children's Publishing Division
1230 Avenue of the Americas, New York, New York 10020
First Aladdin QUIX paperback edition January 2021
Text copyright © 1998 by Joanna Cole and Stephanie Calmenson
Illustrations copyright © 2021 by James Burks
The text of this book was originally published
in slightly different form as *Get Well, Gators!* (1998).
Also available in an Aladdin QUIX hardcover edition.
All rights reserved, including the right of reproduction in whole or in part in any form.
ALADDIN and the related marks and colophon are
trademarks of Simon & Schuster, Inc.
For information about special discounts for bulk purchases, please contact
Simon & Schuster Special Sales at 1-866-506-1949 or business@simonandschuster.com.
The Simon & Schuster Speakers Bureau can bring authors to your live event. For more
information or to book an event contact the Simon & Schuster Speakers Bureau
at 1-866-248-3049 or visit our website at www.simonspeakers.com.
Designed by Heather Palisi
The illustrations for this book were rendered digitally.
The text of this book was set in Archer Medium.
Manufactured in the United States of America 1120 OFF
2 4 6 8 10 9 7 5 3 1
Library of Congress Control Number 2020943554
ISBN 978-1-5344-5257-2 (hc)
ISBN 978-1-5344-5256-5 (pbk)
ISBN 978-1-5344-5258-9 (eBook)

To Ella, Max, and Luke

Cast of Characters

Allie Anderson: Amy Cooper's best friend

Amy Cooper: Allie Anderson's best friend

Gracie Barnes: Bouncy, bubbly, joke-telling friend of Allie and Amy

Marvin Lopez: Dave Wang's buddy

Dave Wang: Marvin Lopez's buddy

Jasmine Hayes: Works at The Candy Basket

Dr. Henry Bogwell: A kind and wacky doctor

Madame Lulu: Fortune-teller who is really Mrs. Suzie Tompkins, a neighbor in Allie's building

Goldie: Amy's goldfish

Contents

1

Front-Page News!

Ring! Ring! The phone rang at **Allie Anderson**'s house. Allie raced to get it.

"Hi," she said.

"Want to go to the playground?" asked a voice at the other end.

The voice belonged to **Amy Cooper**. Allie and Amy were best friends. When they weren't together, they were talking on the phone.

"I need five minutes to get ready and one to get downstairs," said Allie.

"See you in six!" said Amy.

Allie and Amy lived in apartment buildings next door to each other. They each lived on the sixth floor.

Five minutes later, they each

got into their elevators and pressed the first-floor button. They watched the numbers light up. *Six, five, four, three, two, one!*

The girls burst out of their buildings at the exact same time.

"We're amazing!" said Amy.

"You can say that again," said Allie.

"We're amazing!" said Amy.

"Very funny," said Allie. "I'll race you to the playground."

It was a nose-to-nose tie all the way. When they got there, they came to a **screeching** stop. The playground was shut tight, with a big lock on the gate. A sign said:

CLOSED UNTIL FURTHER NOTICE

"Closed?" said Allie. "What are we supposed to do without a playground?"

"It's too horrible even to think about!" said Amy.

"Come on," said Allie. "We might as well go home."

The girls did an about-face.

On the way back, they passed a newsstand and saw a copy of the *Peabody Daily*.

"Look! Front-page news!" said Allie.

The headline read:

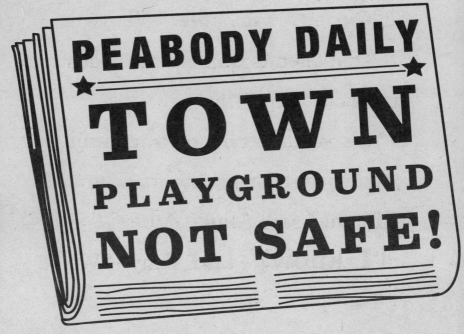

The girls stopped to read all about it.

The report in the paper said the town needed new playground equipment, and there'd be a street fair over the weekend to raise money.

"That means games and rides and food!" said Allie.

"We can have a booth," said Amy.

"Let's do something new and different," said Allie.

"I know!" said Amy. "We

could have a storytelling booth. We'll be good at that."

Just then bouncy, bubbly **Gracie** came along. Gracie always made the girls laugh.

"Hi!" Gracie said. "Did you hear about the fair? We should have a joke-telling booth. I already have a great joke. What did the Ferris wheel say to the carousel?"

"We give up," said Amy.

"See you around . . . and around . . . and around!" said Gracie.

★ 8 ★

The girls rolled their eyes around . . . and around . . . and around.

"We were thinking about having a storytelling booth," said Allie.

"Ooh, that's a good one," said Gracie. "It can be an Instant-Story Booth."

"Cool," said Amy. "Whoever buys a ticket will tell us three facts about themselves. Then we'll make up a fabulous story on the spot."

"Let's try it," said Allie. "Fact number one—"

Whoosh! Before she could finish, she was almost knocked off her feet.

"MARVIN!!!

"Why don't you watch where you're going!" called Allie.

"Why don't you watch where you're standing!" **Marvin** answered.

Marvin could be a lot of fun, but he could also be pretty **obnoxious**.

Whoosh! Something missed Amy's toes by a nose.

"DAVE!!!"

yelled Amy.

Dave had just moved into the neighborhood and was already best buddies with Marvin. Dave came in a close second in the obnoxious department.

"You're blocking traffic," said Dave. "You could get a ticket for that."

"Speaking of tickets," said Allie, "we'll be selling them at our booth."

"What? The goofy-girls booth?" asked Marvin.

"That's so funny, I forgot to

laugh," said Amy. "For your information, we're having an Instant-Story Booth."

"That's so boring, I forgot to wake up," said Dave.

"We're giving skateboard lessons at our booth," said Marvin.

"**Oh really?** Then we'd better have a Band-Aid Booth," said Allie.

"Just for that, we're going to charge you double," said Marvin.

"We wouldn't go to your booth even for free," said Amy.

"Come on," said Allie. "We don't have time to waste. We have places to go!"

"Things to do!" said Amy.

"People to see!" said Gracie.

The three girls linked arms, put their noses in the air, and stomped off.

The truth was, they had no idea where they were going.

2

Gooby Goobs

As they were passing The Candy Basket, they saw **Jasmine**, who worked at the shop, juggling six rolls of Life Savers.

The girls poked their heads in.

"Hi, Jasmine," said Allie. "What are you doing?"

"I'm practicing my act for the talent show at the street fair," Jasmine said.

"A talent show? **I didn't know about that!**" said Gracie. "I can be a stand-up comic. I'd better go write some jokes. See you later."

"What should *we* do in the show?" Amy asked Allie after Gracie had left.

Allie didn't answer. She was in the middle of a yawn.

"We could tap-dance," said Amy.

"No tapping now," said Allie. "My head hurts."

"Let's get some candy. Maybe that will make you feel better," Amy said.

They each got a bag of Gooby Goobs and ate as they walked.

"If you don't want to tap-dance, we can sing. We'll do a **duet**," said Amy. She started to make up a song.

"We sing, we dance.

We jump, we spin!

Watch us now as we begin.

I'm Amy! . . ."

"Come on," said Amy. "You have to sing 'I'm Allie.'"

"I'm not singing," said Allie. "I told you, my head hurts."

"You're being such a grump," said Amy, popping a handful of Gooby Goobs into her mouth. "Mmm, these are so good."

Allie put a Gooby Goob into her mouth, then spit it out.

"**Phooey!** That's gross. I *hate* blue ones," she said.

"You never hated blue Gooby Goobs before," said Amy.

"Well, I hate them now," said Allie. "If you like them so much, *you* eat them."

She handed Amy the bag, then spun on her heel and disappeared down the street.

I wonder what's the matter with Allie, thought Amy, **chomping** on a Gooby Goob. *This blue one tastes perfectly good to me.*

3

Dr. Bogwell

Allie **trudged** through her door.
Her father took one look at her
and asked, "Do you feel okay?"

Allie's mother felt her forehead.
"My goodness! You have a

fever. You're going right to bed,"
she said.

While Allie's mother tucked her
in, her father called **Dr. Bogwell**.

Dr. Bogwell was known for
making house calls with a smile.

"Laughter's the best medicine,"
he told his patients.

In no time, Dr. Bogwell arrived
and rushed into Allie's room.

"Aha! Here's my patient!
Now, where did I put my **tongue
depressor**?" he said.

He reached into his bag and pulled out a teacup.

"No, that's not it," he muttered. He pulled out a rubber chicken. "No, that's not it," he said. Finally he found what he was looking for.

"Please stick out your tongue and say 'ahh,'" said Dr. Bogwell. He held the tongue depressor out to Allie's father.

"**Oops!** Wrong patient," said Dr. Bogwell.

He turned to Allie. Allie stuck out her tongue.

"Blahhh!" she said grumpily.

"Hmm. Let me check your ears," said Dr. Bogwell. "Where's my flashlight?"

He reached into his bag again. He pulled out a tuna sandwich.

"Nope, that's my lunch," he said. He pulled out a deck of cards. "Guess not," he said. Finally Allie heard him say, "Ah yes, here it is."

He shined the light into Allie's ear.

"Amazing! I can see all the

way through to the other side," said Dr. Bogwell.

Allie just groaned. She felt too sick to laugh.

Dr. Bogwell stuck a thermometer into Allie's mouth, then asked, "How are you feeling?"

Allie tried to talk with the thermometer in her mouth.

"Murgle, shmurgle, murgurh," she said.

"Oh my. This is more serious than I thought. She can't even

talk," said Dr. Bogwell, pulling out the thermometer.

"What's she got, Doctor?" asked Allie's father **nervously**.

"She's got a blue tongue, and her temperature's red hot," said Dr. Bogwell.

"A blue tongue?" said Allie's father.

"I ate a blue candy," said Allie. "It was horrible."

"What can we do for her?" asked Allie's mother.

"I'll give you something to get

the fever down. Then she must have one full week of bed rest," said the doctor.

"One week? No way! **I'll miss the street fair!**" cried Allie.

That took every bit of strength she had left.

She woke an hour later. Dr. Bogwell was gone, and she could hear her father talking on the phone.

"I'm sorry, Amy," he said. "Allie's asleep."

"I'm up," said Allie weakly. "Please let me talk."

Allie's father handed her the phone.

"Hi, Amy. I'm sick," said Allie.

"So that's why you were grumpy," said Amy.

"I have to stay in bed a whole week," said Allie. "I can't even go to the fair."

"Oh no! What about our booth? What about our song?" said Amy.

"You can do the booth with

Gracie and sing the song by
yourself," said Allie.

"I can't sing in front of the

whole town by myself! I'm too scared," said Amy.

There was silence at the other end of the line.

"Allie, did you hear me?" asked Amy. "Allie? Allie?"

Allie's mother came on the line. "Allie fell asleep, Amy," she whispered. "She'll have to talk to you later."

As soon as Amy hung up the phone, she felt lost. She was salt without pepper. She was a bat without a ball. **She was Amy without Allie!** What was she going to do? Then Amy had an idea.

4

Fortune Seekers

Amy went straight to **Madame Lulu**'s Fortune-Telling Parlor. It was pink and yellow outside but dark and spooky inside. It was always a little scary going in. Amy stood frozen to the spot. She tried to **remind** herself that Madame Lulu was really Allie's nice neighbor Mrs. Tompkins. That helped.

"Are you there, Madame Lulu? I need you," called Amy from out front.

"Enter, fortune seeker," said Madame Lulu in her **husky** voice.

Amy inched her way inside and was soon sitting face-to-face with Madame Lulu.

Madame Lulu wore a black veil on her head. She had about twenty bracelets on each arm. The bracelets clinked whenever she moved.

Madame Lulu held out her hand. *Clink!*

Amy put a coin into Madame Lulu's palm. Madame Lulu dropped it into her pocket. *Clink!*

"Where's Allie today?" asked Madame Lulu.

"She's home sick," said Amy.

"I'm very sorry to hear that," said Madame Lulu. She gazed into her crystal ball. "It says she'll get better soon. Thank goodness."

"But she has to stay in bed all week," said Amy. "And we were supposed to do a duet at the talent show."

"I guess you'll be doing a **solo** now," said Madame Lulu, grinning.

"It's not a joke," said Amy. "Without Allie, anything could happen. **I might get a frog in my throat!**"

"Let me check my crystal ball," said Madame Lulu.

She pressed her face up close and **squinted** into the glass.

"I see words. But I can't read them. They're too fuzzy," said Madame Lulu, holding out her palm. *Clink!*

Amy handed Madame Lulu another coin.

"Ah, much better!" said Madame Lulu, going into a **trance**. "The crystal ball is puzzled. Do you often get a frog in your throat?

"Well, no," said Amy.

"I heard you gave a great report at school last month," said Madame Lulu.

"That's right," said Amy.

"And you did it by yourself in front of your whole class?" said Madame Lulu.

"Yes. I did pretty well, too," said Amy proudly.

"Then I'm sure you'll do fine at the talent show," said Madame Lulu. **"Wait! Hold everything!** The crystal ball is interrupting us for an important message."

Madame Lulu peered into the ball again.

"It says: 'The show must go on!'" she said.

"You're right!" said Amy. "We need money for the playground. Thank you, Madame Lulu! Thank you!"

5

Listen to This

As soon as Amy got outside, she called Allie.

"Hi, Allie! I just saw Madame Lulu. She said I'll do fine singing a solo. Now all we need to do is finish writing our song," said

Amy. Amy heard Allie's mother

talking in the background.

"Finish your soup, dear," she said. "Then you can talk."

The next thing Amy heard was Allie **slurping**. She held the phone away from her ear. The phone knocked right into—

"MARVIN!!!"

cried Amy.

Marvin **wobbled** wildly on his skateboard.

Dave caught him before he fell.

"Don't tell me you're all alone," said Marvin. "Where's Allie?"

Allie had finished her soup. "I'm here!" she called.

"You're in the phone?" said Dave.

"Yes. For your information, I'm home sick," said Allie. "In fact, I do not have time to talk to goofy guys. I have important **medical** treatments to attend to."

"I'll call you later so we can write the song," said Amy, hanging up.

"What song?" asked Marvin.

"The one I'm singing in the

talent show," said Amy. "What are you doing?"

"We've got a great comedy act," said Marvin. "We're doing our imitation of seasick gorillas."

Before Amy could stop them, Marvin and Dave started beating their chests and making disgusting sounds.

"How's *that* for talent?" asked Dave.

"Talent? All I can say is, good luck at the show!" said Amy.

She turned and went home. She tried calling Allie again, but her call went to voice mail. Amy left a message.

"Call me later!" she said.

She decided to work on the song herself. She went to her room, closed the door, and began to sing.

"We sing, we dance.
We jump, we spin!
Watch us now as we begin.
I'm Amy! . . ."

Amy stopped. It was Allie's turn to say, "I'm Allie."

Uh-oh. This song's no good now, thought Amy. *I'll have to make up a new one that I can sing by myself.*

Amy thought and thought. Then she picked up a hairbrush and held it to her mouth like a microphone.

She needed an audience.

"Goldie!" she said to her gold-fish. "Listen to this!"

"Hello, my name is Amy,
and I'm here all alone.
We need money
for our playground,
so I'm singin' on my own."

Goldie flipped her tail in her bowl. Amy smiled and went on singing.

"We need brand-new swings and monkey rings.
We need—"

Ring! Ring!

"We need a phone?" Amy asked Goldie. "No, wait. That's my telephone."

Amy answered it.

"Hi. Are you ready to write the song?" asked Allie.

"Ready? **I already finished it!**" said Amy.

"You did? Without me?" said Allie.

"Yes! Want to hear it? Goldie loves it," said Amy.

Amy sang the song. With each new line, Allie felt more left out. Not one word of the song included her.

"Nice song . . . for a fish," **mumbled** Allie.

"Huh? Don't you like it?" said Amy.

"I have to go now. I happen to be very sick and need my rest. Doctor's orders," said Allie, and she **plunked** down the phone.

6

Stars of the Show

On the morning of the fair, Allie heard everyone getting ready outside. She went to the window and looked down.

She saw Amy and Gracie

watching the stage get set up for the talent show.

"Hi, Amy! Hi, Gracie!" Allie called out the window. **"I'm over here!"**

But there was so much noise that her friends couldn't hear her.

When the stage was finished, Madame Lulu stepped up to the microphone.

"Gather round, fair-goers!" announced Madame Lulu. "My crystal ball says a great show is about to begin."

The audience rushed to the stage while the performers got ready. Allie saw Amy put on a sparkly bow and bright red tap shoes.

Amy gets to be a star. All I get to be is sick, thought Allie. *Everyone's forgotten me.*

She looked at her old bathrobe and fuzzy slippers. There wasn't a sparkle in sight. Allie got back into bed and pulled the covers over her head. Soon she was asleep.

The talent show went on without her. The audience laughed when Gracie told her jokes. They groaned when Marvin and Dave did their gorilla imitations. And they swayed along with the music when Dr. Bogwell and Madame Lulu danced a **waltz**.

Then it was Amy's turn. There was a big round of **applause** as she went onstage. She looked up at Allie's window. She wished Allie were there to cheer her on.

Amy had two great songs, and

she wanted everyone to hear them—especially Allie.

"*Ahem! Ahem!*" Amy cleared her throat. No frogs were present. She began to sing.

"Hello, my name is Amy,
and I'm here all alone.
We need money
for our playground,
so I'm singin' on my own."

When Amy finished the song, the audience cheered. She looked up at Allie's window. Allie still wasn't there. But Amy had to go on.

"This next song is **dedicated** to my best friend, Allie," she said. Then she sang:

"Allie! Allie! Allie!
I'm so sorry you're sick.
Allie, Allie, Allie!
Please get well quick!"

While Amy was singing, Allie was tossing and turning in her bed. She dreamed that she was all alone and lost in a strange place. Suddenly in her dream she heard her name again and again.

Allie! Allie! Allie!

She opened her eyes and smiled. The voice Allie was hearing in her dream was Amy's real voice, saying, "Everybody sing along!"

Allie jumped out of bed and headed for the window. The next thing Allie knew, the whole town was waving to her and singing:

"Allie! Allie! Allie!

We're so sorry you're sick.

Allie! Allie! Allie!

Please get well quick!"

Allie waved back. She wasn't wearing tap shoes or a sparkly bow. But thanks to her friend Amy, she felt like a star.

7

Insta-Story!

When Amy's performance was over, she and Gracie moved to the Instant-Story Booth right below Allie's window.

"Now you can be part of the booth," called Amy.

"This is so great," said Allie.

"Get your insta-stories here!" called Gracie. "Don't be shy! Step right up!"

A moment later two customers appeared. They were . . .

"MARVIN!!!"

called Allie from the window.

"DAVE!!!"

said Amy from the street.

"We want to hear a story about the two of us," said Marvin,

handing over their tickets.

"Here are three facts," said Dave. "First, we're the coolest guys on the block."

"Second," said Marvin, "we're the coolest guys in town."

"Third, we're the coolest guys

on the planet!" said Dave.

Allie rolled her eyes and called down from the window, "Here's your story: Once upon a time there were two guys. They thought they were the coolest ever."

Amy continued, "They were cooler than wind. They were cooler than snow."

"They were so cool, someone thought they were ice cubes and dropped them into a pitcher of lemonade," said Gracie, bouncing up and down.

"Those cool guys melted away to nothing," called Allie. "And that is . . ."

"The end!" shouted Amy, Allie, and Gracie together.

"Did you say 'the end'?" said Dave.

"That's the best news we've heard yet," said Marvin.

Amy yawned.

"Are we boring you?" asked Marvin.

"No more than usual," said Amy grumpily.

"What's the matter?" asked Gracie.

"I don't know. I'm not feeling so well," said Amy.

Ring! Ring! A few hours later, the phone rang at Amy's house. It was Allie.

"How are you?" asked Allie.

"Terrible," said Amy. "I have to stay in bed one full week, and . . ."

"Amy? Amy, are you there?" said Allie.

There was silence at the other

end. Amy had fallen fast asleep.

After a few days, Amy was feeling a little better and called Gracie.

"Dr. Bogwell just left," Gracie said. "My mother's making me soup."

"Oh no!" cried Amy. "Feel better soon."

When Gracie was a little better, she called Marvin.

"I can't talk right now," said Marvin. "I'm feeling pretty sick."

When Marvin was better, he

called Dave. All Dave could do was groan.

"Welcome to the club," said Marvin.

Two weeks and two dozen bowls of soup later, all five friends were well again. The nasty bug they'd each had was traveling fast, so people were wearing masks to keep each other well.

The friends raced to the playground and burst through the gate.

"The swings are empty!" called Gracie.

"Let's go!" said Dave.

"Race you," said Allie.

The friends ran to the swings, jumped on, and called out together, **"On your mark, get set, *go*!"**

Swinging to the top, they got a clear view of their town's new playground.

"Looking good!" said Allie. "And we helped make it happen."

"Insta-story!" said Amy. "Three facts."

"First, the playground was closed," said Allie.

"Second, we gave our great talents to raise money," said Gracie.

"Third," said Marvin, grinning, "we're the coolest guys at the playground!"

"We're the coolest guys in the universe!" said Dave.

"Arghhh!" said Allie, Amy, and Gracie together.

"How about we're just five cool friends?" said Allie.

"Sounds good to me," said Marvin.

The friends were happy to agree. When they were finished swinging, they raced off to try everything in sight.

Word List

applause (uh·PLAWZ): Clapping to show appreciation

chomping (CHOMP·ing): Biting or chewing in a forceful way

dedicated (DE·dih·kay·ted): Done in someone's honor

duet (doo·EHT): A performance by two people

husky (HUH·skee): Sounding deep and rough

medical (MEH·dih·kul):
Related to medicine or the
treatment of an injury or illness
mumbled (MUM·buld): Spoken
in a way that's hard to hear and
to understand
nervously (NER·vus·lee): In a
worried way
obnoxious (ob·NOK·shus):
Annoying or unpleasant
plunked (PLUNKD): Set down
heavily
remind (rih·MIND): Help to
remember

screeching (SKREE·ching): Sudden, and often noisy

slurping (SLER·ping): Eating or drinking noisily

solo (SO·low): A performance done alone

squinted (SKWIN·ted): Looked at with eyes partly closed

tongue depressor (TUNG dih·PREH·ser): A thin, flat piece of wood rounded at both ends, used to press down on a person's tongue to give a better view of the throat

trance (TRANCE): A sleeplike state during which one is not fully aware

trudged (TRUJD): Walked slowly with heavy steps

waltz (WAHLTS): A dance for two people moving together to a certain beat, going around the dance space

wobbled (WAH·buld): Moved unsteadily

Questions

1. If you were at the fair, what would your booth be?

2. What would you do at the talent show?

3. Can you make up an Instant Story? Here are three facts: Something in your neighborhood is missing. Two investigators are on the case. There will be a big reward when the item is recovered.

4. What would you do to cheer up a friend who was sick?

5. Allie and Amy's plan got turned upside down when Allie got sick. Has a plan of yours ever suddenly changed? What did you do?

C UCKLE YOUR [XXXX] THROUGH THESE EASY-TO-READ ILLUSTRATED CHAPTER BOOKS!